The Very Best Pumpkin

written by Mark Kimball Moulton   illustrated by Karen Hillard Good

A PAULA WISEMAN BOOK

Simon & Schuster Books for Young Readers

New York London Toronto Sydney

This story is dedicated to all the future pumpkin farmers,
most especially Aiden, Logan, Lee, Evan, Cameron, Sophia, and Lola.
—M. K. M. and K. H. G.

SIMON & SCHUSTER BOOKS FOR YOUNG READERS

An imprint of Simon & Schuster Children's Publishing Division

1230 Avenue of the Americas, New York, New York 10020

Text copyright © 2010 by Mark Kimball Moulton

Illustrations copyright © 2010 by Karen Hillard Good

All rights reserved, including the right of reproduction in whole or in part in any form.

SIMON & SCHUSTER BOOKS FOR YOUNG READERS is a trademark of Simon & Schuster, Inc.

For information about special discounts for bulk purchases, please contact Simon & Schuster Special Sales at 1-866-506-1949 or business@simonandschuster.com.

The Simon & Schuster Speakers Bureau can bring authors to your live event. For more information or to book an event, contact the Simon & Schuster Speakers Bureau at 1-866-248-3049 or visit our website at www.simonspeakers.com.

Book design by Lucy Ruth Cummins

The text for this book is set in Alcoholica.

The illustrations for this book are rendered in watercolors, instant coffee, and bleach.

Manufactured in China

0510 SCP

10 9 8 7 6 5 4 3 2

Library of Congress Cataloging-in-Publication Data

Moulton, Mark Kimball.

The very best pumpkin / Mark Kimball Moulton ; illustrated by Karen

Hillard Good.

p. cm.

"A Paula Wiseman Book."

Summary: While Peter carefully tends a special pumpkin on his

grandparents' farm, quiet Meg watches from her new home next door.

ISBN 978-1-4169-8288-3 (hardcover)

[1. Pumpkins—Fiction. 2. Friendship—Fiction. 3. Farm life—Fiction.]

I. Good, Karen Hillard, ill. II. Title.

PZ7.M8613Ver 2010

[E]—dc22

2008046639

*D*own a winding country lane and over a rolling hill, you'll find Pumpkin Hollow Farm, where a young boy named Peter lives with his grandparents, Mimi and Papa.

In the spring they grow plump, juicy strawberries, and in summer, corn, crisp and sweet as honey, but it's in the fall that Mimi and Papa's farm produces the most wonderful crop of all . . .

Pumpkins!

Big pumpkins, small pumpkins,
short pumpkins, tall pumpkins—
they grow pumpkins of every shape
and size!

One summer not so long ago,
as Peter was tending his pumpkins,
he spotted a long, curlicue vine he
hadn't noticed before.

It twisted and traveled all the
way beyond the far edge of the
field. Curious, Peter followed
where it went. . . .

Cautiously he clambered over pumpkin after pumpkin

as he trailed the vine into the nearby meadow.

And at the vine's very end, much to Peter's surprise, he
discovered a tiny pumpkin growing all by itself among the weeds.
Poor little pumpkin, thought Peter. *It's awfully lonely out here.*

Carefully Peter cleared the weeds so the pumpkin could enjoy some sunshine. Then he loosened the soil around the plant and gave it some water.

Every day that followed, when Peter had finished tending all the other pumpkins that grew side by side in the field, he hurried out to the meadow to visit his lonely little pumpkin.

Peter was so busy that summer, he didn't notice that a new
family had moved in next door to Mimi and Papa's farm.

Peter's new neighbor, Meg, spent most of her time alone,
reading under a tree at the far edge of her yard.

One afternoon, as Meg was reading, she heard a noise in the meadow next door. She peeked around just in time to see Peter as he bent to care for his special pumpkin.

Day after day Meg quietly watched, and little by little Peter's pumpkin grew.

It grew larger and larger and rounder and plumper and began to change color from pale yellow to dark green and finally to a deep, rich orange-red that glowed in the late summer sun.

It was the most beautiful pumpkin Meg had ever seen!

Soon the leaves began to change, and the days grew shorter and cooler. Folks began to arrive at Mimi and Papa's farm to select their pumpkins.

Peter helped his teacher, Mrs. Clark, choose a pretty little pumpkin for her desk at school.

Peter proudly showed Officer Bailey a big pumpkin in the middle of the field. It would look dandy on the steps of the police station in town.

Miss Jane, the librarian, thanked Peter after he helped her pick just the right pumpkins for her award-winning pies.

Peter helped pumpkin after pumpkin find a good home, but he was saving one pumpkin . . .

HayRides

TAFFY APPLES

cornmaze

his special pumpkin.

The best pumpkin of all.

Late one afternoon Meg and
her parents came by the farm to
pick their pumpkins.

Peter watched as Meg stepped
gingerly into the field and began
to search.

She peeked under giant leaves
and crawled over rambling vines
and carefully stepped between
pumpkin after pumpkin, but
couldn't seem to find just the
right one.

Meg looked here and she looked there. She looked everywhere.

Just as she was about to leave, someone stepped up behind her.

"I think I might know where to look," Peter said.

Peter guided Meg past all the pumpkins in the field
until they came upon the wandering vine. "Follow me," he
said. They followed the vine to the meadow where Peter's
pumpkin grew.

"This one's the very *best* pumpkin," said Peter.

"Oh, it's beautiful!" Meg cried.

Meg shyly told Peter how she'd been there all along
watching him care for his pumpkin.

"I knew you were there," Peter confessed. "That's why
I'd like you to have it."

Together Meg and Peter carried their special pumpkin
across the field to show Meg's parents.

Autumn turned into winter and winter into spring.

Soon it was summer once again, and Peter was busy tending a new crop of pumpkins side by side with his new friend Meg.

Every day they cleared the weeds and tilled the soil and watered the field.

And just like the pumpkins, their
friendship grew and grew and grew.

The End

Peter's guide
TO GROWING YOUR OWN
Very Best Pumpkin

Growing pumpkins is easy and fun!

First decide what kind of pumpkins you'd like to grow. Your local garden center should have just the seeds you're looking for.

Choose a sunny spot in your garden where your plants can spread out, and prepare the soil by adding in lots of organic ingredients like compost.

Mound the soil into a small hill (about one foot high, two to three feet across), flatten the top, and then plant your special pumpkin seeds at the proper depth, according to the package—usually about an inch. Water well.

Just like Meg and Peter, tend your pumpkins throughout the season, keeping your plants free of weeds and remembering to water them during dry spells.

Before you know it, your pumpkin plants will begin sending out long trailing vines, then flowers will form, and, come fall, you'll have your own very best pumpkin.

Jack-O'-Lanterns for carving.

Pie pumpkins are delicious.

Heirloom varieties look pretty.